Dear Reader,

Antonia is the story of a family that has to leave their lovely home to find safety elsewhere. This is what is happening in Colombia, my country, to many farmers, and to Black and Indigenous people. These families have to leave their towns to go to live in big cities, because their land has been taken from them by people or companies who plan to use it for their own profit.

Even in difficult situations, you can find happiness and have fun when your loved ones are around. You can make new friends. You can laugh. We all have problems, and I think it is easier to go through them when we stay positive and brave.

DIPACHO

This book is dedicated to all those who have been forced to leave their homes.

ANTONIA
A JOURNEY TO A NEW HOME

DIPACHO

a maria russo book
minedition

NIÑO CHÉVERE

iANTO

minedition

A division of Astra Publishing House
North American edition published 2021 by mineditionUS

Text and Illustrations copyright © 2021 by DIPACHO
Coproduction with minedition Ltd., Hong Kong
Rights arranged with "minedition ag", Zurich, Switzerland. All rights reserved.

mineditionUS, 19 West 21st Street, #1201, New York, NY 10010
e-mail: info@minedition.com
This book was printed in March 2021 at Hong Kong Discovery Printing Company Limited.
3/F., Blue Box Factory Building, 25 Hing Wo Street, Tin Wan, Aberdeen, Hong Kong, China
Typesetting in Booster Next FY
Library of Congress Cataloging-in-Publication Data available upon request.

ISBN 978-1-6626-5045-1
10 9 8 7 6 5 4 3 2 1
First Impression

For more information please visit our website: www.minedition.com